Tilly Beany

and the
Best Friend Machine

Tilly Beany
and the
Best Friend Machine

Annie Dalton
Illustrated by Kate Sheppard

EGMONT

*This book is for
Asha Kumari Chauhan Field,
who wanted more
stories about Tilly,
and for Sophie and Maya*

EGMONT
We bring stories to life

First published in Great Britain in 1993
by Methuen Children's Books Ltd

This edition published in 2004
by Egmont Books Ltd
239 Kensington High Street
London W8 6SA

Text copyright © 1993 Annie Dalton
Illustration copyright © 2004 Kate Sheppard

The moral rights of the author and the illustrator have been asserted

ISBN 1 4052 0057 X

3 5 7 9 10 8 6 4 2

A CIP catalogue record for this title is available from the British Library

Typeset by Dorchester Typesetting Limited and
Avon DataSet Ltd, Bidford on Avon
Printed and bound in Great Britain
by the CPI Group

Contents

The Best
Friend Project

When Tilly Beany went back to
school after the summer holiday, her
big sister Kate had to take her.
Tilly's mum worked in the mornings
now.

Tilly was so excited to have
Kate to herself she didn't even mind
about going out in the rain.

But they'd only walked as far as
the post box when they saw a boy
with a bashed-up looking bike
waiting for them on the corner. The
boy's hair stood up in soft spikes
like a baby's, and he wore a long
thin green jumper with holes in it.
His legs were long and thin, too,

1

inside their jeans. Tilly thought he looked like one of Anil's stick insects.

When Kate saw the boy she went bright pink. And even though Tilly pulled the worst faces she could think of, Kate still let the stick-insect boy dawdle beside them all the way to the gate of Tilly's school. And all the time his bike creaked, squeaked and groaned as if it was going to fall to pieces any minute.

Tilly was so furious she ran off into the playground without saying goodbye. Stupid Kate and that stick-insect boy had nearly made her late on her first day.

But the moment she burst through the classroom door she forgot all about Kate. Standing by Miss Hinchin's desk, twiddling the coat buttons on her smart red coat, was a new girl.

Tilly Beany cheered up at once. She cheered up enormously. They'd never had a new girl in the class before but Tilly knew as soon as she saw her that they were going to be very good friends.

Miss Hinchin clapped her hands.

'Bernice has come to join the class,' she said. 'And we want to help her to feel at home with us, don't we children? Stephanie dear, perhaps you'd like to show Bernice round the school?'

But Stephanie didn't get out of her seat. She just hid her face, giggling. Bernice stared at the ground, still twiddling her buttons. Tilly could have died.

Miss Hinchin sighed. 'Stephanie's feeling rather shy,' she explained. 'Who's going to show Bernice where we hang our coats and where we go for our dinner?'

But the other children stayed glued in

3

their seats, staring at the new girl as if she was some kind of space creature.

Tilly felt sorry for her. She even felt a bit sorry for Miss Hinchin, whose neck was turning red. If Mrs Grosgrain, the headmistress, walked past, she'd think Miss Hinchin's class had been turned into statues.

Someone had to do something and Tilly Beany knew who that someone had to be. She put on her sensiblest expression and marched right to the front.

'I'll show her round, Miss Hinchin,' she said, beaming.

Their teacher gave Tilly a disappointingly small smile. 'What a kind girl, Tilly,' she said. And her voice wasn't as friendly as it could have been. 'But don't take too long. We're starting a very important new project today.'

Tilly didn't know why it was, but no matter how helpful she tried to be, Miss

Hinchin never really seemed to *like* her much. Even though Tilly hadn't been anyone at all but the same ordinary real old Tilly Beany for months and months now.

Tilly took Bernice to the cloakrooms and showed her where to hang her coat and shoebag. Bernice's peg had a sunflower picture beside it.

'I had a watering can at my other school,' Bernice said.

Tilly liked her soft, husky voice. In fact Tilly Beany liked everything about her exciting new classmate. Bernice's dark brown eyes reminded her of shiny, flat toffees. Her thick lashes were as black as liquorice.

Bernice even *smelled* like something nice to eat, Tilly thought; a warm, sweet smell.

'We go right across the playground when it's dinner-time, but don't worry, I'll show you where,' said Tilly importantly.

The rain shower was over. The puddles

had bits of sky floating in them.

'There might be a rainbow,' shouted Tilly over her shoulder. She was enjoying having the new girl to look after. 'Come on, this is where we go.'

She held the door of the big hall wide open so Bernice could peep in. They could hear the cooks bashing giant saucepans about on the other side of the serving hatch.

'We can smell the dinner when we're doing singing,' explained Tilly. 'Chocolate pudding's my best. You get lovely sauce.'

'We're vegetarian,' said Bernice, pulling a face as if she didn't much like the smells

wafting from the kitchen. 'My mum gives me a packed lunch.'

'Sophie wanted to be vegetarian,' Tilly said, beaming. 'But she hates all the vegetables, that's the only problem. I've got two sisters actually. Kate's the funniest. I've got a brother too, Tom. He makes our bathroom smell like wet dog, my mum says.'

Tilly meant for Bernice to tell her stories about *her* brothers and sisters next but she didn't. The new girl didn't say another word, just went on walking silently back across the bright wet playground.

By the time they were indoors again, Tilly's breath was beginning to sound uncomfortably loud and wheezy inside her ears.

'I bet it's scary being new,' Tilly said at last.

'Oh, I'm used to it,' said Bernice in an airy way. 'We move house all the time. My mum says we have gypsy blood. Our new

7

house is ever so big. It's got a pond with fish.'

Tilly had lived in the same too-little house ever since she was born. It was rather a tight squeeze now the four Beany children were growing so big.

Tilly's sisters were lucky. They shared a room with each other. Tilly had to share a bedroom with Tom and his awful socks.

The Beanys didn't have a pond either. And she was fairly sure they didn't have gypsy blood.

But smiling her sunniest smile, to show that Tilly Beany was still tremendously worth getting to know, Tilly said, 'You can sit at our table with me and Stephanie. Do you want to?'

'All right,' said Bernice.

But she didn't smile back. Bernice hadn't even smiled once yet.

She was probably just shy, Tilly thought. She almost wished her brother was here.

That was one good thing about Tom, he knew loads of funny jokes. Tilly could nearly remember the one about the jellyfish, but trying to get the words right inside her head made her feel horribly shy herself. Tilly hadn't ever been shy before. At least, not since she was very very small.

The only sound in Tilly's ears as they walked back down the corridor, apart from her own breath squeezing loudly in and out, was the clop-clip of Bernice's shiny new shoes and the scuffle-scuffle of Tilly's old sandals.

'Oh there you are, Tilly,' said Miss Hinchin. 'I was just going to send a search party. Children, this term we're going to start an exciting project all about –' she paused to make sure everyone was listening properly – 'FRIENDS. Now everyone wants a special friend of their very own, don't they? So what kind of person would you like as your special friend – erm – ?'

Miss Hinchin looked around, deciding who to ask.

Tilly waved her hand. Her shyness had worn off now. She wanted to tell everyone she had a special friend already. But Miss Hinchin didn't seem to see Tilly. Instead, she picked Steven who didn't even have his hand up!

'Tell us about your special friend, Steven,' Miss Hinchin said in a soft kind voice. Steven hated answering questions in class. That's why Miss Hinchin always asked him loads, to help him get over it.

Steven looked at the floor and growled something. It was always hard to hear what Steven was saying except when he was showing off with the other boys. Then he was as noisy as a zoo.

'Speak up, dear,' said Miss Hinchin in her encouraging voice.

'Miss,' said Natalie helpfully. 'Miss, Steven said his guinea pig's *his* best friend, Miss.'

Everyone giggled. Steven's ears went bright crimson.

'That's nice, dear,' said Miss Hinchin kindly. 'And I'm sure we'd all like to hear about Steven's guinea pig later, wouldn't we? But animals are really only *pets*. Only people can be our special friends.'

'Ow, Miss,' complained Anil. 'I was going to say about my stick insect. He's called Bruce, Miss.'

Tilly shot up her hand again.

'Joe,' said Miss Hinchin firmly, looking right through Tilly as if she was a ring doughnut and not a person at all. 'Do you know what kind of person you'd like for your special friend?'

Tilly sighed. It was only the first day back but she was wishing it was home-time already. Maybe she'd turned invisible without knowing it? Even when Tilly was being specially helpful, grown-ups often simply didn't seem to see her.

'I want a brown friend, Miss,' Joe said at once. 'A brown boy just like me, because he wouldn't call me names.'

Miss Hinchin looked horribly embarrassed to hear this. 'Oh, I'm quite sure we never have that sort of name-calling in this school,' she said quickly. 'But it doesn't really matter what people look like on the outside, does it, Joe? It's the inside that counts. So what would be the *really* important thing about your special friend?'

'I just *told* you, Miss,' said Joe sternly. 'Brown skin.' Then he folded his arms, shut his mouth tightly and stared at the floor like Steven.

'Miss, people sometimes call me names too, Miss,' said Pritesh.

'And me,' shouted Adam unexpectedly.

12

Joe scowled. 'You're not brown, silly.'

'Glasses,' said Adam, tapping his spectacles sadly. 'And goofy teeth.' He shrugged his shoulders right up to his ears. 'They call me "Bugs Bunny".'

Nathan sniggered and pushed Steven off his chair.

Their teacher was looking as if *she* was wishing it was home-time now. Tilly could see Miss Hinchin hadn't meant anyone to talk about guinea pigs or goofy teeth. She certainly didn't want them to mention name-calling and brown skin.

What *did* Miss Hinchin want to say, Tilly wondered. And if she wouldn't *tell* the children what she was thinking of, how could they help her?

'Miss, Miss – I wouldn't like a friend who only liked me for my money, Miss,' called out Shazna helpfully. 'Like that man in *The Tinder Box*, Miss.'

'That's right, Shazna. Good girl,' said Miss Hinchin, looking a little happier now, even though Shazna hadn't put up her hand politely first. 'We all want our friends to like us for ourselves, don't we?'

Alice put up her hand, giggling like mad. Usually Miss Hinchin didn't approve of giggling, but today she saw Alice right away.

'I wouldn't like a friend who was *exactly* like me, Miss,' said Alice, hardly able to speak for laughing. 'Suppose we got muddled up when we played hide-and-seek and I had to go back to her house to live and she went to live with my mum and dad, Miss.'

All the children laughed except for Bernice. Miss Hinchin had a quick look at her watch to see if it was playtime.

Tilly was bursting. Miss Hinchin was going to cheer up as soon as she heard about *her* friend. 'Miss Hinchin,' she shouted out happily. 'I've got a really special friend actually. She's very old and she's called Miss Gladwell. I have tea with her on Wednesdays and we dress up as pirates and robbers and –'

'Thank you, Tilly,' Miss Hinchin interrupted in the specially firm voice she often used for Tilly. 'But an old lady can't really be a little girl's best friend, can she? Think of someone closer to your own age, dear.'

'Stu-pid,' hissed Nathan, poking Tilly from behind. 'Stupid baby.'

Tilly went hot all over. She shut her mouth tight to stop any other stupid words leaking out by mistake. You were supposed to learn things at school. But there must be something wrong with Tilly because Tilly often felt as if she was *unlearning* them instead. All kinds of things which seemed perfectly simple when she was by herself at home, somehow got muddled up in Tilly's head after Miss Hinchin had explained them.

Nathan must be right. Tilly Beany thought unhappily. She *was* a stupid baby if she didn't even know what 'friend' meant.

By playtime Stephanie had nearly stopped being shy. She let Bernice try on all her bracelets. Bernice shared some of her home-made flapjack. Tilly shared her crisps too. But after this little picnic the three of them stood around awkwardly. No one seemed to know what to say. Tilly's breathing was so loud in her ears again she was afraid she'd go deaf.

'It's really boring here,' Bernice said suddenly in her soft, husky voice. 'It was better at my old school.' And she glowered at Tilly as if it was her fault.

Tilly felt ashamed. She wanted to make school fun for Bernice, but she couldn't think how. She had been *trying* to think of interesting games to play but as soon as she told them to Bernice they turned as boring as school rice pudding.

For something to do, Stephanie picked up a dirty old acorn and put it in her pocket.

Tilly had an idea. 'Pretend that acorn's magic,' she said excitedly. 'There's three magic acorns in the kingdom and we've got to find them.'

'How will we tell the magic ones, though?' asked Stephanie. Stephanie was never very sure about magic.

'By the tingling in our fingers of course,'

said Tilly, happy again. 'We're three princesses and our father's dying. He's the king. And we've got to journey far and wide to find the magic acorns to save him.'

Tilly started to be a princess right away. She was the youngest one, who found the magickest acorn of all. She began to glide gracefully across the playground, her head held high because of her golden crown. But when she glanced round to see where the other two had got

to, they hadn't moved an inch. Stephanie was showing Bernice a trick tattoo she'd got out of a comic.

'Come on,' called Tilly. 'Hurry up or the king will die.'

'We're not playing,' Stephanie bawled. 'Bernice doesn't want to.'

'Well *I'm* journeying far and wide anyway,' Tilly called defiantly. She stalked away, holding her head higher than ever, so no one would guess about the sad prickly feeling in her insides.

The new girl liked Stephanie best.

Maybe Bernice and Stephanie were even going to be best friends.

Before today Tilly had never thought about having to have one special friend. Suddenly she saw that everyone else in the world went around in twos, just like the animals in her old wooden ark.

Her mum and dad. Sophie and that giggly girl Rose, she phoned to talk about boys. Tom and his weird friend Merv.

And Kate – well, Tilly had a feeling

19

Kate wanted to be a two with the silly stick-insect boy.

Only Tilly was left out. Like that terribly long song with numbers in that Mrs Grosgrain made them sing, 'Green grow the Rushes-oh'.

'One is one and all alone and ever more shall be so,' Tilly sang forlornly.

Tilly wondered if there was something very wrong with you, if no one wanted to be your special best friend.

She looked around the playground. It seemed larger than usual. Alice was playing mothers and fathers with Shazna. Pritesh and Anil were being galloping horses with a stolen skipping rope. Steven and Nathan kicked a lopsided ball

with a puncture in it.

Very casually, Tilly glanced across to where Bernice and Stephanie stood under the trees. Stephanie was whispering in Bernice's ear. A smile spread across Bernice's face. Then the new girl actually giggled.

Tilly's lonely prickles turned into a tight hurting feeling in her chest.

Could they be whispering about her?

Ever since playgroup Stephanie had followed Tilly around, admiringly pulling on her sleeve, whispering in her ear, copying every single thing Tilly did. It drove Tilly mad, but somehow she'd got used to it.

Now Stephanie was looking admiringly at Bernice. She slid her arm around the new girl's neck so their heads were close together, one shiny brown and one curly fair head, as they whispered again.

Then Bernice looked right at Tilly and laughed.

For a whole minute Tilly Beany couldn't

breathe. She could hardly even see, she was so hurt.

But she wasn't going to let it show.

Instead she stared at the sky in a thoughtful way. She even hummed a tune. Tumty tum tumty.

Two birds sat on the roof of the hall enjoying the sunshine. Even birds went round in twos, Tilly thought. But still she hummed.

Suddenly Stephanie was beside her, pulling at Tilly's sleeve. 'What are you doing?'

Tilly wanted to hug Stephanie then, only Bernice was right behind her.

'I was only looking at those birds,' Tilly said calmly. 'I think they're going to make a nest in a minute.'

Bernice pulled a face. 'Birds don't make nests in the autumn, silly.'

'That really depends on the bird,' said Tilly in her most scientific voice. 'Some birds in *this* town prefer to make their nests in the middle of winter.'

Stephanie was amazed. 'What do they make them out of?'

'Er – snow of course,' said Tilly quickly. 'They hammer little weeny igloos out of it with their beaks. It takes absolutely days and days.' She pressed her lips together, looking very hard at Bernice to see what she'd do.

Bernice began to giggle. 'You're making that up,' she said. 'You silly, silly thing. Birds don't make igloos!'

Suddenly Tilly burst out laughing too. She laughed so hard the tears came splashing down her face. The three of them stomped around the playground together arm in arm, laughing until the whistle went.

After playtime Miss Hinchin wanted them to crayon pictures of their best friends. Tilly asked if she could do her sister Kate. She'd nearly forgiven Kate for the stick-insect boy.

But Miss Hinchin said a sister couldn't possibly be a best friend.

Tilly picked up a crayon and put it down again. She had a quick look round. Most of the other children were looking around too, to see what they were meant to be doing.

All except for two.

Anil who was stubbornly crayoning something long and thin and green. And Bernice. Her crayon was flying over the paper until she caught Tilly looking. Then she covered her drawing with her arm so Tilly knew right away that Bernice wasn't drawing *her*.

'I'm drawing my *real* friend Janine from my other school,' said Bernice.

Stephanie sucked her little finger, frowning. 'Had I better draw you then?' she whispered to Tilly. 'I'll draw you, Tilly, if you'll draw me.'

Tilly didn't think this could be right. Stephanie had just been giggling with her arm round Bernice's neck!

'Sorry, I'm drawing a best friend you don't know about, Stephanie,' said Tilly in a faraway sort of voice. She picked up a crayon and began to draw. 'I was just trying to think how to draw her long, long beautiful hair.'

As Tilly drew she was telling herself a story about the girl in her picture.

The girl's name was Nina. She was a gypsy princess and lived in her own painted caravan and wore flouncy skirts and bright shawls with fringes. She had dangly gold earrings and gold necklaces. Nina knew how to throw knives and ride a pony bareback. She had loads of friends. Some were old and some were very young. Some of them were even gypsy kings and queens. Nina thought it was perfectly fine to have friends who were birds and animals.

But the best thing about Nina was that of all her friends in the world, she liked playing with Tilly Beany most of all.

'Please Bring a Bat'

Tilly and Stephanie were going to Bernice's home after school, to help think up spooky ideas for her Halloween party.

Tilly had been looking forward to it all day. Tilly was brilliant at thinking up party ideas. But when they reached Bernice's house, Bernice and Stephanie went off by themselves, giggling. Tilly tried going after them, but they just ran away.

'Don't you care about the party now?' asked Tilly, following them, puzzled.

'No, we're too tired, aren't we, Bernice?' said Stephanie.

27

And she went into fits of giggles again.

But Tilly knew you had to plan a party properly, or no one had any fun. She sighed. It looked as if Tilly was going to have to organise everything by herself. So in the end it was Tilly Beany who thought up the bats, the scary skeleton invitations and the Bad Dream Cake with the black icing.

It was Tilly who asked Bernice's mum if she'd make some spooky biscuits, exactly like the dog's bones in the *Funnybones* book.

And it was Tilly who found the big black pot (which only had boring old houseplants in it) and asked Bernice's mum if they could borrow it for a cauldron.

And what were Bernice and Stephanie up to while Tilly was doing all the work? Rolling around the floor, giggling and tickling each other, that's what.

Tilly couldn't understand Bernice at all. Sometimes she was Tilly's friend and sometimes she wasn't. She changed every

time the wind blew, Tilly thought. And
Stephanie was an old copycat so *she*
changed every time Bernice did.

Tilly wanted to be friends *every* day. But
one day Bernice and Stephanie were both
funny and nice to Tilly, the next day they
acted as if she had turned into a very bad
smell. Sometimes they actually stopped
being friendly right in the middle of a good
game for no reason at all! She never knew

where she was.

And now, even after all Tilly's hard work, those silly gigglers were acting as if she wasn't there at all. First, Tilly felt angry with them, then she was scared. Perhaps she'd really gone invisible this time.

She ran off to find Bernice's mum. She saw Tilly straight away, which was a relief, so Tilly told her the party plans instead.

Bernice's mum said things like: 'That's very clever, Tilly,' and 'What an extraordinary imagination.' This was the kind of thing Miss Hinchin usually said to Tilly. But the words sounded quite smiley when Bernice's mum said them. Tilly stayed chatting happily to her in the cosy kitchen until Kate came to take her home.

But next day at school Bernice told everyone her mum had a headache from listening to Tilly talk so much. And Stephanie said *her* mum thought Tilly was miles too big for her boots anyway. It was because she was the youngest. Youngest children were always spoilt.

Tilly wanted to die. She never wanted to go to Bernice's house and see that smiley mother again. But if she didn't go to the party Bernice and Stephanie might be more unfriendly to her than ever.

If only Tilly could be in a proper two with a special best friend of her own, she wouldn't care what anyone said. The trouble was, now Mum was busy with her new job, and Kate was going out with the stupid stick-insect boy, Tilly Beany wasn't sure that even her family remembered about Tilly any more.

Once Miss Gladwell told Tilly she should show everyone how special Tilly

Beany really was. But Tilly didn't feel special any more. She felt left out and lonely.

On Halloween Tilly was walking to Bernice's house (as slowly as possible) with her mum, when they saw Miss Gladwell posting a letter.

'Tilly,' Miss Gladwell called. 'I was coming to visit you, but you look as if you're going to be busy.'

Tilly turned pink as a tulip under her green slime. She'd promised Miss Gladwell she'd mostly be the ordinary Tilly now. And here she was in the street wearing a sinister cloak, a spooky hat and her face all over green!

'I'm going to Bernice's party,' Tilly called back.

32

She rushed up to her friend waving her invitation, so she'd know Tilly wasn't a fibber.

Miss Gladwell smiled and Tilly noticed her eyes weren't as twinkly as usual. Miss Gladwell looked tired. 'I've come without my glasses, Tilly,' she said. 'You tell me what it says.' The old lady's voice was tired too.

'Bernice is new,' explained Tilly. 'When she was *really* new, me and Stephanie had to look after her. I helped do the invitations. That's a skeleton, look. See those letters. PBAB.' Tilly pointed her witchy green nail. 'That means "Please Bring a Bat". I brought loads of bats anyway.'

She fished in her pocket. 'Black cut-out spooky ones to hang up and scare people. Squidgy red jelly ones to eat. They're the creepiest. They wibble when you shake them.' She shook the jelly bat under Miss Gladwell's nose.

The old lady took a step backwards laughing. 'I believe you, Tilly!'

Tilly stopped wibbling her bat. Underneath her friendly smiles, Miss Gladwell looked terribly sad. Tilly's lip trembled. What could be wrong?

'We'd better go, Tilly,' said Tilly's mum. 'I'll bring her on Wednesday as usual, Miss Gladwell.'

'That's why I wanted to see you,' said Miss Gladwell unhappily. 'My sister's ill. There's no one else to look after her. I'm afraid Tilly and I can't have our special teas for some time.'

Tilly forgot to breathe, she was so shocked.

Miss Gladwell's sister lived in America. You had to fly across the sea to get there. Miss Gladwell's house would be empty. No pointy-blunt shoes to go tip-tapping over the polished floor. No dreamy music on the old record player. No one to spin the glass ball in the window and send rainbows swirling round the room. And no one to make delicious Wednesday teas for Tilly.

'I'm sorry,' said Miss Gladwell gently. 'I'm going to miss you, Tilly.'

'Tilly understands,' said Tilly's mum. 'We hope your sister gets well soon.'

Tilly wanted to be polite and grown-up just like her mum, but she couldn't manage to make her voice work properly yet so she just nodded. There was a sudden pain in her middle, as if Miss Gladwell's shocking words were little knives wriggling round inside her trying to get out.

'Bye,' Tilly Beany managed at last in a croaky voice.

But Miss Violet Gladwell had tip-tapped away into the dark by then, in her beautiful swishy coat, and it was too late.

The first time Miss Gladwell visited the

Beanys, Tilly was being Cindertilly. Being someone else wasn't exciting any more, only she didn't know how to stop and be the ordinary Tilly again. No one in the family knew what to do with her until Tilly's dad remembered Miss Gladwell.

Tilly thought Miss Gladwell was a fairy godmother but she was really Kate's dancing teacher and not magic at all. Yet somehow the old lady still made everything turn out happily for Tilly Beany, like a real fairy story.

Miss Gladwell knew Tilly needed someone who enjoyed the other exciting Tillies who lived inside her as much as Tilly Beany did herself! Then she could be the ordinary Tilly *most* of the time, without getting too muddled up.

And that's how the Wednesday teas began.

Now Miss Gladwell was going away, Tilly was scared she'd get muddled again.

She dug her witchy nails into her jelly bat. She wasn't going to cry like a spoiled old baby. If Kate was poorly, Tilly would fly across the sea to look after her too. Not if it was grumpy Sophie though, she decided. Only Tilly's mum could stand being anywhere near Sophie Beany when *she* was ill.

Tilly's mum squeezed her hand (the one without the bat). 'Perhaps Bernice will be your friend now,' she said. 'You had a lovely time planning this party, didn't you?'

Tilly tried to smile but her face felt too stiff. She hadn't told her mum about the Best Friend Project or how Tilly was the only person in the world not in a proper two. She hadn't told her mum what happened at Bernice's house either. She'd have died of shame.

Tilly sighed a wobbly sigh and her face grew hot under its witchy green with remembering. She wasn't going to say a

word at Bernice's party anyway. Tilly
Beany had made up her mind to be as silent
as the Little Mermaid in the story, until it
was time to go home, so no one could say
she gave them a headache.

When they got to Bernice's house,
Stephanie was already trotting up the path,
wearing a droopy cardboard cone on her
head like an upside-down ice cream cornet.
She'd stuck stars on it so people would think

it was a witch's hat, but the glue hadn't worked so the stars were coming off. She was wearing the same pinafore dress she'd worn all day at school.

Stephanie put a big smile on her face when she saw Tilly. 'Tilly, you look like a real horrible witch!' she squealed.

Tilly's tummy gave a lurch. 'I'm not in the right mood for this party,' she whispered to her mum. 'But I do have to go, don't I?'

'You certainly do,' said Mum firmly. 'After you made me buy all those bats. What's the matter, Tilly? You love parties.'

'Probably I'm growing out of them,' said Tilly hopefully.

The other children were arriving now. Nathan came charging past in a skeleton suit, miles ahead of his mum, yelling, 'Trick or treat!'

Tilly thought Nathan was too bulgy round the middle to be a skeleton.

'Sophie's coming to fetch you,' Mum

said, giving Tilly a pat on her bottom to encourage her to follow the others.

But Tilly stayed where she was, scuffling her feet. 'Ow – why not Kate?'

'Kate's going out with Ollie Pyke.' Ollie was the stick-insect boy. 'Off you go and have a lovely time!' called Tilly's mum, who was in a hurry to pick up some dry-cleaning.

Tilly trudged up the path towards Bernice's front door. It took ages. Her legs felt stuffed with wet sand. Through the door a pumpkin lantern grinned its yellow toothy grin. Bernice and her mum were in the hall welcoming everyone. Bernice wore velvet leggings, furry mittens for paws and a pair of little soft furry ears. Someone had drawn elegant whiskers on

either side of her nose.

Tilly wanted to stroke Bernice's front paws, they looked so sweet.

Bernice squealed like Stephanie when she saw Tilly. Then she said, 'Ooh sorry, Tilly, I thought you were an ugly, slimy old witch.' Bernice smiled, a sweet little pussy-cat smile to go with the paws.

'My *real* best friend is coming to this party,' she told Tilly, so Tilly knew she didn't mean the smile. 'Her dad's bringing her specially. Her name's Janine. Don't you wish that was *your* name, Tilly?'

Tilly shook her head dumbly.

'Don't you? Why not?' Bernice looked annoyed. Almost as if she enjoyed making Tilly jealous, Tilly thought.

'Because it's a soppy girly name,' Tilly burst out to her own surprise, forgetting all about

41

being silent like the Little Mermaid. 'And I'm an ugly old slimy old witch, *that's* why. Ha ha.'

And with a swirl of her sinister cloak Tilly stalked past to find the party.

Bernice's big brother Henry was in charge of apple-bobbing. The apples danced up and down like rosy red corks in the water. Nathan was the first to try to catch an apple in his mouth.

Everyone stood round watching Nathan splosh rivers of water over the kitchen floor. The other children were so quiet and shy, Nathan's piggy snuffles echoed very loudly inside the bowl.

Except for the flickering candles the kitchen was dark. Eerie shadows drifted across the walls. It was *almost* spooky, Tilly thought reluctantly. Something bumped her face. She squeaked with fright. Then she saw the trick spider dangling on its long thread in front of her. Tilly Beany glared. It took more than a trick spider to scare *her*.

Tilly was glad she had her ugly witch face on. No one could see what she was thinking under her slime. She could glare and mutter as much as she liked. It was perfectly normal for witches to be rude.

She knew Sophie wouldn't come to fetch her for ages. Sophie was always late for everything. Tilly found a deep dark chair in a deep dark corner and curled herself up as small as possible, hoping she could get through the party without anyone noticing her.

The kitchen was getting rather wet now so Bernice's mum made the children stop bobbing for apples. She wanted them to bite doughnuts off long strings hanging from the ceiling instead, only they mustn't use their hands. Bernice jumped up and down in her leggings, waving her soft paws and mewing like a pussy cat when it was her turn.

But everyone else was strangely quiet.

Not partyish at all.

Bernice's mum went round with the flowerpot cauldron full of gingerbread bones trying to cheer everyone up. When she got near Tilly, Tilly tried to make herself even smaller.

'Tilly, dear, I didn't see you sitting there so quietly,' she said. 'Would you like some gingerbread?'

Tilly shook her head. She could see no one remembered the funnybones were her idea.

'Aren't you feeling very well, dear?'

Tilly nodded to show she was feeling quite well, thank you.

'Have you lost your voice?'

But luckily someone called Bernice's mum away so Tilly could go on sitting in her corner without anyone bothering her.

'Come *on*, Sophie,' she whispered into her hand, so no one else would hear. 'Hurry up.'

Then someone tugged Tilly's sleeve.

'Hey – you must be my twin!' said the someone, giggling.

Tilly turned to see who it was and jumped with surprise.

It was another witch!

Only this one was smaller and not quite so slimy.

Then Tilly had an even bigger surprise.

'I'm Janine,' said Tilly's witch-twin.
'Who are you?'

Tilly stared at Bernice's real best friend,
not knowing what to say. She almost said a
witch name because that would have been
more fun, but she'd promised Miss Gladwell
so she quickly told her real name instead.

'It's a really boring party, isn't it?' said
Janine. 'I didn't want to come, but Mum
said I had to.'

There were so many thoughts whizzing
round Tilly's head she still didn't know what
to say. Janine didn't seem to *know* she was
Bernice's real best friend. And Janine was
nice, Tilly thought in surprise, not girly at
all. A smiley feeling started up inside Tilly
Beany. As if she didn't actually want to sit
in a dark corner and be dumb like the Little
Mermaid any more. And suddenly Tilly
found her tongue.

'They should play funny games,' she

said excitedly. 'And tell scary stories.'

'Tell me some funny games then,' said her witch-twin, giggling.

'The Witch's Glue Pot of course,' said Tilly. *She* was giggling now.

'Hey, everyone,' Janine shouted. 'We're going to play the Witch's Glue Pot. It's loads of fun! How do you play it?' she whispered to Tilly.

Everyone wanted to play, even Bernice.

Tilly and Janine were the only real witches at the party (Stephanie had taken off her droopy cornet) so they had to catch the other children and drag them back screaming to the enormous glue pot.

Then everyone had to try to escape.

Bernice's dad came home while they were playing and took pictures of them with his camera. Everyone was hot and giggling now and no one was a bit shy any more.

Not even Tilly Beany.

'Now let's tell the spooky stories,' said

Janine when everyone was worn out. 'How do we start, Tilly?' She smiled a big friendly smile at her witch-twin.

Tilly felt a tiny warm sun come out in the middle of her chest.

Janine *liked* her!

'It's easy,' said Tilly. 'We sit on the floor in a circle, with just one candle to make it *really* spooky and everyone takes turns to say a little bit of the story.'

So everyone sat down and Bernice's mum carefully placed one flickering candle in the middle of the circle where no one could knock it over.

Nathan looked worried. 'What story do we tell?'

'You make it up,' explained Tilly. 'It has to be a scary one.'

Nathan said he didn't know how to make up stories.

'It's my party,' said Bernice promptly. 'So I'll start. Once upon a time there was a beautiful black cat who lived in the middle of a magic wood . . .'

Bernice was quite good at stories, Tilly decided. When Bernice got to the most exciting bit of the story she stopped, the way she was supposed to, and someone else had to take over.

Gradually, as if the story they were telling together was a clever magic spell, Tilly forgot she was in Bernice's kitchen.

Instead she was floating through the woods under old enchanted trees. By the time Henry finished his part, about a wicked giant, everyone was looking nervously over their shoulders.

Now it was Tilly's turn to be the storyteller. She took a big breath. But before she could say a word, someone hammered loudly on the back door. Then an enormous shadow spread itself slowly right across the wall.

Everyone screamed, even Bernice's mum.

'It's the giant!' squeaked Stephanie. 'He's coming to get us!'

But it was only Sophie with her friend Rose.

'No one heard me knocking so I came round the back,' Sophie said. 'I didn't mean to scare everyone.'

She bent down and whispered in Tilly's ear. 'Mum was worried. She said you seemed really sad. So I came early.'

But Tilly wasn't at all sad now!

'Ow,' she sulked. 'I was having a good time.'

'OK, no need to be mouldy, me and Rose will wait for you,' said Sophie unexpectedly.

'Why don't you girls help yourself to some gingerbread and join in,' suggested Bernice's mum.

So they did.

Then, after the party was properly over, Rose and Sophie took Tilly home, swinging her wildly between them all the way, singing at the tops of their voices.

Tilly giggled at the shadows they made in the dark street.

Two stomping giant girls and a funny little witch flying through the air!

Tilly's mum and dad were out so Rose and Sophie had to help Tilly wash her slime off.

'You were good fun at the party, Sophie,' said Tilly, sounding surprised.

'Hurry up,' said Sophie impatiently. 'Me and Rose want to watch a video.'

'You want to talk about boys,' said Tilly, wiggling her finger in the air. 'That's what you want.' She started to pull her baggy witch's dress off but it got stuck over her head. 'Help,' Tilly yelled, 'I can't see.'

She danced madly about, trapped inside the dress. Small objects came raining out of her pockets. Even though her head was still muffled in the dress, Tilly grovelled on the floor trying to pick the things up.

At last, somewhere near her foot, Tilly's hand blindly found a strange, slithery something. Then another.

What *could* they be?

'Oh, come on,' said Sophie crossly. 'Get a move on.'

'Oh, it's my bats!' yelled Tilly in a bandaged sort of voice. 'It's my jelly bats! I brought them back home by mistake.'

Rose rescued Tilly from inside the dress. 'You can eat them while you're waiting to go to sleep,' she said.

'But I've brushed my teeth,' said Tilly, looking hard at Sophie.

She didn't want Sophie telling tales to Mum.

'Just this once then,' said Sophie, sighing.

So Tilly sat contentedly in her cosy bed by herself until she'd eaten every one of the jelly bats *very* slowly.

And she knew she really deserved them.

Airy Mary
and Holly Dark

One Saturday near Christmas,
Sophie drifted into the Beanys'
kitchen wearing a big old black
T-shirt instead of a nightie, her long
hair over her face. 'It sounds like a
zoo down here,' she growled. 'Why's
Tilly yelling?'

Sophie hated people talking
before her eyes were open. Sophie's
eyes never opened till she'd had her
morning cup of coffee.

Tilly Beany couldn't wait
that long.

'No one will tell me what's in
Daddy's letter,' she shrieked. 'Just
because I'm the littlest. And I found
it on the mat anyway.'

'We were trying to discuss what was *in* it,' Mum explained to her.

'But it's not fair,' Tilly yelled. 'Dad showed *you* the letter and *you* showed Kate and Tom. But *nobody* showed me.'

'We were just going to –' began Tilly's dad.

'Don't I still belong to this family?' Tilly inquired coldly. 'I haven't turned into a tiny little black beetle, have I?'

'Of course you belong to this family,' Dad sighed. 'And you're much, much too noisy to be a little beetle –'

'So why doesn't anyone discuss anything with *me*, then?' Tilly

stamped her foot, her eyes filling with tears.

No one ever understood how dreadful it was for Tilly being the youngest.

Sophie held her head, groaning. 'Tell Tilly whatever she wants to know,' she croaked. 'She's making the china rattle.'

Dad gave in. 'We've been invited to spend Christmas on a farm, Tilly.'

Tilly was so astonished she couldn't say a word, but her eyes went very round and green.

'The Martins' little girl, Lizzy, is a bit younger than you, Tilly,' Dad went on. 'But quite big enough to play with, I should think.'

Tilly's eyes sparkled again. She'd forgiven her mum and dad now. She'd forgiven absolutely everybody.

Lizzy Martin was going to be her special friend! Tilly knew it as soon as she heard her name. She even knew what her new friend looked like.

Lizzy wore colours so zingy and bright she looked as if she'd been dipped in the rainbow. Mostly she wore a big dressing-up hat with a pink rose on it, except when she had to go to school. Lizzy's friendly face was exactly like Tilly's own, but her eyes were as blue as cornflowers instead of green, and her cheeks were all over freckles. And Lizzy's favourite kind of game in the whole world was pretending, just like Tilly's. That's why she wore the hat with the rose.

Tilly didn't mind now about not having a special friend at school.

A holiday friend was miles more exciting.

'I want to go,' she declared at once. 'I want to meet Lizzy.'

'You've met her,' said Mum. 'But you were both in nappies at the time. And Lizzy was as bald as an egg.'

Tom did his annoying donkey laugh, 'Hyaw-hyaw.'

'Why do people always talk about nappies,' snapped Tilly. And she started tidying the table very fiercely to show everyone how grown-up she was now.

'So – are we going to the Martins' for Christmas?' Dad asked, grabbing his cup before Tilly could throw his coffee in the sink.

Sophie peered through the tangles of her Saturday-morning hair. 'Christmas?' she said, appalled. 'With the Martins? Is that what you're all yelling about? Well, *I'm* not coming.'

But she did of course.

The Beanys had never packed a whole Christmas into their car before. When Tilly tucked her own friendly strawberry pillow

into the boot, she caught a glimpse of holly-patterned paper and shivered with excitement.

Tilly had never spent Christmas away from home either.

As the car pulled away she said, 'We brought my stocking, didn't we? I'm going to open mine *exactly* the same time as Lizzy.'

Dad smiled in his driving-mirror. 'Everything's under control, Jellybean. Don't worry. You and Lizzy can open your stockings together on Christmas morning. Now snuggle down and get some rest. It's a long, long drive to the north.'

'You're telling me,' sulked Sophie. Sophie hated the country. Too smelly and not enough streetlights.

Tilly must have been tired without knowing it because when she woke up she got a shock. They were in the north already!

The sky was a strange greenish colour with a single star hanging in it, bright and clear as an icicle. And all around were the barest, loneliest hills Tilly had seen in her life. There wasn't even one little tree anywhere, only smashed-up bits of rock scattered messily about. Other smaller rocks poked bony elbows through the thin covering of grass, reminding her of Ollie Pyke.

Then Tilly rubbed her eyes.

'Daddy, those stones are *moving*.'

'I think the moving ones are sheep,' explained her dad.

The sheep stared back at Tilly with silly cartoon faces. Some of them had twisty horns like little handlebars. Their wool hung shaggily down their sides, lumpy with mud and bits of gorse.

Tilly was disappointed. In books, sheep looked clean and fluffy like brand-new jumpers. But she liked the streams gushing over stones in the cold green twilight, and the way some of them turned into waterfalls on the way down.

As the sky grew darker the waterfalls seemed to hang magically in the air like wisps of white smoke. Tilly gazed at them until her eyelids drooped again.

When she woke everything was pitch black and silent. For a scary minute Tilly thought she was all by herself.

Then a dog barked nearby making Tilly jump.

Sophie yelled, 'Ow, that's my eye.'

'Oh, Soph,' said Tilly, relieved. 'You're here.'

Kate gave her hand a squeeze in the dark. 'We're all here, Tilly,' she said. 'And this is Holly Tree Farm.'

Lights went on everywhere and a door flew open. Tilly saw a row of muddy boots and a half-grown puppy running around, waving its tail like a flag. Stumping down the path with a torch, was a big man in a huge red jumper, his breath making frosty clouds.

It was Dad's friend, Dan Martin.

'Put the kettle on, Jess!' Dan shouted into the house. 'The Beanys are here.'

The Martins' house wasn't like any houses Tilly was used to. The floors were made of stone and none of the carpets reached the edges of the room. When Jess Martin opened the door to bring in the supper, gusts of freezing air blew everywhere.

Tilly shivered so much her teeth rattled. Even the dangerous-looking fire, roaring and snapping away in the open hearth, couldn't keep out *this* cold. She pulled her jumper up round her nose. 'Is this a North Pole house, then?' she asked, in a muffled voice.

'That's right,' said Dad's friend, with a serious face. 'I hope the noise of the reindeer on the roof won't keep you awake, Tilly.'

'Reindeer?' said Tilly, amazed. 'Really?' But everyone burst out laughing so she knew Dan was only joking. Tilly quickly leaned against her mum for comfort, her eyes prickling. She hated that teasing kind of grown-up joke and when she grew up she was never going to tease *anyone*.

'Behave, Dan,' Jess scolded. 'Let her get used to us.'

The puppy was roaming round, snuffling up crumbs like a little hoover and knocking things over with his tail. Everyone kept shouting, 'Sit *down*, Albert', but Albert was still only little so he kept forgetting.

Even if there weren't any reindeer, the north seemed very different indeed to Tilly. Her hot milk tasted funny and the air was full of strange smells; the clean washing on the big wooden airer, the sharp smell of the wood fire, the onions in rustling bunches over her head.

Albert smelled too. He smelled of dog biscuit and something else.

Tilly sniffed his fur as he bumped against her, hopefully licking her face.

Poo, *he* smelled of scorched puppy!

Ben Martin laughed. Ben was almost the same age as Tom. 'Albert burned his bottom last week,' he told her, showing her Albert's frazzled behind. 'If we didn't have a fireguard for Lizzy, he'd sit *in* the fire if he could. He's a proper hot dog, is Albert.'

Tilly giggled. Ben was nice. But she hadn't even seen her special friend Lizzy yet. She peered hopefully around. I bet she's excited, just like me, she thought.

Then Tilly Beany noticed a small someone peeping shyly from behind a chair.

'Come on out and say "hello", Lizzy,' said Dan.

The someone tiptoed a little way out of the shadows.

Tilly's heart dropped right down into her boots.

Lizzy Martin wasn't wearing a dressing-up hat with a rose. She didn't have freckles and her clothes weren't bright at all. Everything about Lizzy was pale.

Her hair was the palest kind of fair. Her eyes were the palest kind of blue. She looked exactly like a grubby little fairy except instead of a fairy's dress, Lizzy was wearing a tatty sleepsuit. Only her cheeks were bright and they were as pink as carnations.

Suddenly the little girl hid her face and ran out of the room.

'Lizzy's shy,' said Jess. 'She doesn't get to meet many new people.'

But she's a baby, Tilly thought indignantly. Lizzy Martin was much too little and babyish to be Tilly's special Christmas friend. She probably didn't even go to *school* yet.

To cover her disappointment, Tilly yawned. 'Can I go to bed?' she asked her mum. 'I've had a terribly tiring journey, haven't I?'

But the bed was strange too. Tilly's bed at home was full of cosy lumps that fitted her shape exactly right. She had to climb right up into this one before she could even lie down. And even once she was safely there, the mattress wibbled scarily about like a boat on the water every time she moved.

After a while Sophie came to share the wibbly boat-bed. She said she had a headache, but Tilly had already heard Mum mutter about 'sulking' to Lizzy's mum.

'I don't know if I like the north,' Tilly whispered. 'Do you wish we'd stayed home, Soph? I do.'

Either Sophie was asleep already or she was sulking so hard, she wasn't even talking to Tilly. But Tilly preferred to sleep with a sulky Sophie than all by herself in this strange, uncomfortable, funny-smelling house. So she patted Sophie's cross, bony back through its T-shirt.

'Goodnight, my dear,' she said softly. 'Sleep tight. Hope the reindeer don't bite.' She giggled a little to herself in the dark. Then she fell asleep.

Before they even had breakfast next day, Ben took them to feed the calves. Tilly stroked their heads and stood very still while the littlest calf licked her fingers with its rough, lolloping tongue. When it wasn't looking she wiped her hand on her coat to get the dribble off.

After breakfast everyone helped to decorate the tree and hang up holly and mistletoe. When they'd finished, the house smelled green and secret, like a forest, and Sophie forgot she was meant to be sulking. She and Kate made mincepies and Tilly helped Jess with the shortbread and baking bread. Tilly had to put careful patterns in each round of dough with a big silver fork, exactly the way Jess showed her.

Now she'd got used to them, Tilly
thought the Martins were lovely.

Except for disappointing Lizzy.

'It's a shame Lizzy's so little,' Kate said
to Tilly when no one was listening. 'Dad
must have got muddled up.'

But Lizzy wasn't only little. She was also peculiar, Tilly thought. Peculiar and *rather* rude.

All morning Lizzy went skipping about the farm like a grubby fairy in her faded frock with faded flowers all over it, a pair of muddy old wellies on her feet. And the whole time she had private conversations with herself in a little grouchy old lady voice.

At first (even though Lizzy was so disappointing), Tilly tried to join in. If Lizzy liked pretending so much, Tilly knew loads of ways to make it more fun.

'If you want to be a princess or something,' said Tilly helpfully, 'I saw some lovely paper in a cupboard we could use for crowns.'

But Lizzy simply flitted away like a little faded butterfly, as if Tilly hadn't said a word, and started muttering to herself again.

Most peculiar.

At dinnertime Tilly noticed something very strange indeed. Because Lizzy was so small she had two extra cushions on her chair so she could reach the table. But beside Lizzy's chair was *another* chair with two extra cushions on it.

When Lizzy's dad set the table, he set a spoon, a fork and a plate just like Lizzy's, right in front of this empty chair, just as if he was expecting another child to sit in it.

When Lizzy's mum gave Lizzy her dinner, she put some dinner on the plate next to Lizzy's.

Tilly was wild with curiosity to see who the extra dinner was for. But no new child appeared to climb up into the empty chair and everyone just got on with eating.

Tilly Beany was mystified.

Lizzy said in her grouchy little old lady voice, 'You've forgotten Mary's water, Mummy.'

'Oh, sorry, so I have. Silly me,' said Lizzy's mum.

And she poured water into a glass and set the glass beside the plate! Lizzy cocked her head as if she was listening to someone. 'Mary says "thank you", Mummy,' she said, and she smiled a grouchy little old lady smile.

'Well, see she doesn't spill too much gravy on the cloth,' said Lizzy's mum, but as she said it she pulled a face at Tilly's mum. And she dished up more roast potatoes for Tilly's dad as calmly as if nothing unusual had happened!

Tilly's eyes were like saucers. So *THAT* was who Lizzy had been talking to all morning.

She nudged Tom. 'Tom, *Tom*,' she hissed. 'I think one of the children in this family is invisible.'

Tom gave her a strange stare, but Jess was a wonderful cook so he was too busy eating to answer.

Tilly looked round the room.

Everyone was still acting quite naturally, eating, chatting, pouring water. Just as if they hadn't noticed that mysterious, empty chair.

Maybe having invisible children was one of those things grown-ups all knew about but that it was very rude for anyone to mention.

Tilly wondered if Mary Martin had been born invisible, or if she'd *grown* invisible later. Tilly had never met any invisible people. But she'd heard about them in stories. They usually got *made* invisible with a wicked spell, she remembered. Sometimes they put on a special cloak to make themselves invisible so a wicked giant wouldn't see them. But Tilly was fairly sure Mary's invisibility wasn't the cloak sort.

Tom was busy talking to Ben about football so Tilly nudged Sophie this time. 'Have you heard of anyone having invisible children, Soph?' she whispered.

Sophie shook her head until she'd swallowed her mouthful. 'Never,' she said. 'Why?'

'Just wondered,' said Tilly casually. 'Maybe it only happens in the very north places or something.'

Dan Martin was clearing invisible Mary's plate away now. Most of the dinner was still left on it, Tilly noticed. Probably invisible children didn't need so much food as the visible kind.

Unless –

A new and terrible worry slithered like a caterpillar into Tilly's mind. She inspected her fingers anxiously. They *looked* as solid as usual. But suppose the people who were *turning* invisible couldn't tell what was happening to them until it was too late to change back?

Tilly Beany felt shivery, remembering how at school Miss Hinchin didn't always seem to see her.

Suppose being invisible was like an extra special thinness that came and went at first, like that awful rash Tilly had once, before you were finally stuck with it.

Tilly hoped it wasn't too late. 'Lots of pudding for me, please,' she said quickly as Jess dished up the trifle.

'This fresh air is giving you quite an appetite, Jellybean,' said Tilly's dad, surprised when Tilly asked for a second big helping, minutes after the first. 'If you eat much more your buttons will pop off.'

The trifle made Tilly so full she knew she wasn't going to turn invisible just yet. Not until ages after Christmas anyway.

But she was still terribly anxious about Mary Martin.

How ever did your mum and dad hug you if they couldn't see you?

And how would they *find* you if you got lost in a big Woolworths, the way Tilly had once? Perhaps Mary had a special little song she had to sing, so they could *hear* where she was, or a tiny bell she wore on a ribbon. That's what Tilly would do.

'I suppose they have to go to a special school too,' she murmured to herself.

'Who do?' asked Tom. '*What* school? What *are* you muttering about, Tilly?'

'An Invisible Children School, of course,' hissed Tilly. 'Don't shout, Tom. I don't want to hurt her feelings, do I?'

Later everyone shared the washing-up and putting away and everyone except Lizzie sang carols and silly songs.

Even grumpy Sophie.

Jess's face looked so bright and happy as

she sang.
Tilly couldn't
bear it.

'Lizzy's
mummy's
terribly brave
I think,' Tilly
murmured to
her mum, as
they hung the
tea towels to
dry on a
funny pulley
thing that
swung high

up to the farmhouse ceiling.

'Brave? About what?' asked Mum,
surprised.

'Because – you know, about her – *other
little girl*,' Tilly whispered, after she'd made
sure no one else was listening.

'Other little – ? But there's only Lizzy.'

Tilly twisted her hands together. 'I mean –'

She looked around again quickly. 'I mean Mary. The one who sits in that chair.' She pointed. 'The *invisible* one.'

Tilly's mum stared at her. 'Oh, Tilly, you must mean Lizzy's imaginary friend!' And she started to laugh.

'Oh, I didn't know,' said Tilly, bewildered. 'What does that mean?'

Mum quickly put her arm round Tilly. 'Lizzy spends too much time by herself. She doesn't have any friends her own age and because she was so lonely, she made one up. To Lizzy, her friend seems absolutely real. She has to have her own chair and her own plate and spoon –'

Tilly felt sorry for Lizzy. She knew how it felt to be lonely. But she also felt a bit annoyed. It didn't make sense for Lizzy to keep on playing with some old pretend friend, when a real live friendly Tilly had come to stay!

Then Tilly had an idea.

'Oh, no,' said Dad, catching sight of
her. 'Your eyes have gone very round and
very green, Matilda Beany. That must
mean trouble.'

'No, it doesn't, Daddy,' Tilly promised.
'It's a nice idea. You'll see.'

And she ran to whisper something to
Lizzy's mum so no one else could hear
her plan.

At tea-time Lizzy climbed up into her
chair as usual, made herself comfy on her
pile of cushions and checked that Mary had
her share of sandwiches.

Then she looked puzzled.

Squeezed between Tilly and Tom's chairs
was a new chair. In front of this chair was a
new plate, cup and saucer. And when
Lizzy's mum passed round the sandwiches,
she popped one on to the mysterious
new plate!

'Who else is coming to tea then?' Lizzy asked her mum in her old lady voice.

'Oh, just a friend of mine actually,' Tilly called across to her. 'Your mum said it was all right for her to come.'

Lizzy frowned. 'She wasn't here before.'

'Yes, she was,' explained Tilly. 'She came with me in the car. But she's shy so she didn't dare have dinner with us but I said she wouldn't get any presents, so she came in. Didn't you, little one?' She smiled fondly at the chair and gave it a second sandwich.

'Presents,' said Lizzy thoughtfully. 'Do you mean Christmas presents?'

'Yes, I'm doing her stocking after tea. She's really excited.'

Lizzy bit into her sandwich, still looking doubtful. 'What's her name then?'

'Er –' Tilly looked around the room. 'Holly,' she said quickly. 'Holly – er.' She caught sight of the uncurtained window. The winter darkness outside looked friendly with the Christmassy room reflected in it.

'Holly Dark,' she said. 'Holly's very lonely,' Tilly explained to Lizzy. 'She doesn't mind me as a friend to be going on with, but she'd rather have a special friend who was invisible just like her. Then they could play magicky games together, the sort invisible children play. Do you know, when invisible children play pretend games, they don't even have to dress up!' She beamed at Lizzy. 'They just *turn* into anything they want to be. Tigers, princesses, clowns.'

Lizzy ate the rest of her sandwich in silence. Then she said, 'My friend's just called Mary. She hasn't got two names like your one.'

'You could call her Airy Mary if you wanted,' said Tilly daringly. Lizzy took a mincepie, frowning.

'Because she's invisible,' Tilly explained. 'So it's quite a good name, *I* think.'

'Airy Mary,' said Lizzy as if she was testing it. 'It sounds like that baby old song,' she added thoughtfully. 'Airy Mary, quite contrary.' Then, to everyone's amazement, Lizzy actually giggled.

When tea was over Lizzy and Tilly helped clear away.

'Where does Holly live then?' Lizzy asked Tilly. And her voice wasn't nearly so grouchy this time.

'Oh, just in a tall tree,' said Tilly calmly. 'In a very special tree house. She hangs beautiful lights in it so people can see it for miles and miles. Where does your friend live?'

Lizzy thought for a moment. 'She used to live in my bedroom, but the other day she thought she'd try living in a tree so she's just moved.'

'Does yours wear her nightie all the time?' asked Tilly. 'Holly does. She thinks it's stupid getting dressed.'

'So does mine,' said Lizzy. 'But she likes wearing a crown when she wants to be smart. At Christmas anyway.'

'I saw some little wooden pegs in your kitchen,' said Tilly. 'With funny heads on. We could make Christmas dollies for them.'

'We could wrap them up,' said Lizzie excitedly. 'And borrow my dad's big woolly socks to be their stockings.'

'We could hang the socks up,' said Tilly. 'And jingle a little bell to be the sleigh bells.'

'Come upstairs with me to get the socks though,' said Lizzy. 'It's a bit spooky in the dark.' She reached for Tilly's hand and together they raced for the stairs.

But on the dark draughty landing, Tilly suddenly froze.

'*Look*,' she whispered, pointing. 'Don't move. Can't you see them?'

Lizzy's eyes grew huge. 'Oh, Tilly,' she whispered back, seeing the funny little shadows flickering against the wall. 'It's Holly and Mary! I can see their *crowns*. And *they're* holding hands too.'

'It's Christmas magic,' Tilly explained in a very soft voice so as not to frighten the shadow children away. 'It's very special. They wanted us to see them because they're

so happy to know they can play together all Christmas.'

'Hey!' called Lizzy's mum from downstairs. 'What happened to my helpers?'

Tilly's dad grinned. 'Christmas magic,' he told her. 'There's a lot of it about. Maybe you'd better give me that tea towel to be on the safe side.'

And Tilly's dad started to dry the forks and spoons instead.

Tilly and the Best Friend Machine

The Beanys should have been happy to get back to their own warm comfortable house when their country Christmas was over, but they were not.

Not even Sophie.

'I hate this messy old place,' she raged. 'There's never any room for *my* things. Tom just dumps his stuff everywhere.' She was trying to hang up her jacket, but there were two coats, three scarves and an anorak on the hook already so her jacket kept falling off.

Kate was trying to talk to Ollie on the phone. 'Oh, stop *looming*, Tom,' said Kate crossly. 'There's *nowhere* private in this house.'

'Actually there is *one* place,' Tom began, grinning, but everyone yelled, 'Oh shut up, Tom.'

'I wish I'd stayed with the Martins,' Tom sulked. *'They* didn't pick on me all the time.'

'We do need more coat hooks, you know,' said Mum to Tilly's dad. She said it in a cupboardy sort of voice because she was trying to get a pile of plates out of the kitchen cupboard at the same time. The Beanys had bought fish and chips on the way home.

Mum wiggled the cupboard door in the special way that was the only way to make it shut properly. *'And* new cupboards,' she added. *'And* about ten gallons of paint,' she sighed, catching sight of the dirty scuff marks on the kitchen walls.

She plonked Tilly's plate on the table in front of her.

Tilly looked at her supper in surprise.

The wonderful cooking smell had
made her mouth water hungrily
while she and dad were waiting
in the chip shop for the chips to
finish frying. And the
chips had
looked golden
brown and
tempting as
they came out
of the sizzling
oil. But now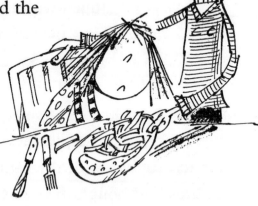
they looked pale and greasy. The chip shop
magic had somehow worn off on the
way home.

Tilly's dad shook his head. 'New coat
hooks won't do it,' he said. 'Or cupboards.
Or paint. I'm afraid we've just grown out of
this house. It needs someone new to love it
and we need somewhere bigger. After
staying with the Martins it's like coming
back to a poky little box.'

'I'm not living in the country,' said Sophie at once. 'I like crowds and exhaust fumes. I'm a town girl, I am.'

Dad didn't answer her. He was looking so worried Tilly knew he was thinking about money again so she felt worried too.

'Mum, these chips are all cold and soggy,' Tom complained.

'Oh, do stop *moaning*, Tom,' yelled everyone, though they'd all been thinking the same thing.

'Be like that,' said Tom, hurt. 'I'm never talking to any of you ever again.'

'Suits me,' said Sophie spitefully.

'And me,' said Kate. 'I never knew why we needed a brother anyway.'

'For crying out loud, *all* you kids shut up so your mum and I can eat in peace,' yelled Dad.

So the Beanys sat in their shabby dining-room eating their cold fish and chips in miserable silence.

But Tilly was the miserablest Beany of
them all. For one thing Dad had yelled
at her, too, and she wasn't even *saying*
anything. Worst of all, now she was back
home, she'd remembered about
school again.

Tilly still hadn't found a special friend.
What was she going to do?

Next day Tilly carried an extra chair
to the dinner table and asked her mum for
an extra bowl of home-made soup. All
through the meal Tilly chatted to the empty
chair beside her and took little sips out of
the extra bowl when she thought no one
was looking.

Once she said to her mum in a grouchy
little old lady voice, 'You've forgotten to give
Holly her water.'

And when Tom was humming while they
were washing up afterwards she said nastily,
'Holly hates that stupid song anyway.'

But next day Tilly took the extra chair

away again.

'The trouble is,' she said to Kate, 'Holly never tells me anything back. It's boring having a pretending friend, *I* think. Only nobody real wants to be friends with me, that's the problem. And I haven't even got a puppy like Albert. Or a kitten like Mum used to push around in her doll's pram.'

Tilly's face crumpled. Fat tears squeezed out of her eyes even though she was blinking them hard.

'Poor old you,' said Kate, hugging her little sister. 'Can't I be your special friend?'

Tilly wriggled away, and she folded her arms across her chest. 'Not really, Kate,' she said sternly, 'You're a sister, not a friend. Anyway you're in a two with Ollie Pyke. *I* need to be in a two with somebody special.'

But just then Mum came in looking pleased with herself. She'd been on the phone for ages. 'Cheer up, Tilly,' she said. 'Your worries are over. You and I are going on a Big Friend Hunt.'

'When?' asked Tilly nervously.

'Right now, if you like,' said Tilly's mum. 'School isn't the only place to make friends, you know. I've been phoning everybody I know with children your age.'

And right away Tilly's mum took her to visit someone from work who had a boy who was in the infants, like Tilly.

The boy was called Michael. Michael's house was tiny and tidy. It had a tiny tidy garden at the front and a twiddly iron gate that took a nip out of Tilly's thumb when she closed it. The windows shone so fiercely in the winter sunlight it hurt Tilly's eyes to look at them so she still had her eyes screwed tight shut when Michael's mum opened the door.

But as soon as she got inside Tilly saw
that the house was the specially clean kind,
and not meant for children at all. There
were strips of plastic laid along the carpet to
stop dirty footprints, even though no one
was allowed to wear shoes in the house!

Tilly felt shy and bare in her too-small
pink spotty socks that Mum was always

putting in the drier
by mistake.

'Are we meant to
play on those little
plastic paths,' she
whispered to her
mum. 'The problem
is, what if I slip off?'

But Michael's
mum said she was
meant to play
upstairs quietly in
Michael's room.
So Tilly and

Michael found themselves frowning at each other in the middle of Michael's small clean tidy bedroom.

Michael was small, clean and tidy too. He smelled a little bit of nice shampoo, Tilly noticed, and a little bit of that purple drink you spit with at the dentist's.

'Why are you here?' Michael asked at last, with a puzzled expression.

'Oh, to play and stuff,' said Tilly airily. She knew Michael wasn't going to be her special friend. His room was as tidy as a grown-up's.

'What games do you know then?' asked Michael.

'Pirates, robbers, princesses,' said Tilly, counting them off on her fingers. 'And Lost in the Jungle, and Journey to the Golden City of the Stars.'

Michael looked even more bewildered. 'My parents haven't bought me those games yet,' he said.

'They're pretending games, silly,' Tilly explained. 'You don't buy them from a shop. You make them up out of your head.'

Michael didn't understand about making things up. And the more Tilly tried to show him, the more worried he became.

In the end they played picture dominoes. Tilly was so bored she kept forgetting it was her turn. Even after they'd played the game hundreds of times it was still too early for Tilly to go home, so for a change they played *Snap*. To make it more interesting, Tilly pretended she was a prisoner in a tower with nothing to do but play *Snap* all day. She didn't tell Michael, though, in case he got worried again.

'Have *you* got a special friend, Michael?' she asked after a while.

(The room felt terribly quiet and she thought *someone* ought to say something.)

'No, but I've got a special pet. It's not the usual kind, though, Tilly,' explained

Michael. 'Promise not to laugh if I show you?'

She nodded encouragingly. So the little boy took a snowy-clean white handkerchief out of a drawer and began unfolding it very carefully. 'People often think I'm strange,' he said, and worried crinkles came into his forehead. The handkerchief was nearly unfolded now.

Tilly backed away. 'It isn't something dead, is it?' Merv had tricked her with a dead mouse once.

Michael looked shocked. 'Don't be silly,' he said. And he held out what looked like a very large, stripy humbug. When Tilly saw what the humbug-thing was, she did blink, just once, with surprise. But she caught herself before the surprised feeling turned into giggles because she didn't want to hurt Michael's feelings.

'It's a stone,' Michael explained very gravely. 'And stones *can't* die, you know, so

you can keep them forever if you want to.
I found this one in our garden. It doesn't
make a mess like usual pets so my mum
doesn't mind it living in my room. I'll find
you one if you like. Then you can tell your
troubles to it at night. That's what I do,
don't I, stone?' He stroked the stripy stone
tenderly.

'Thank you,' said Tilly politely. And to
be friendly, *she* gave the stone a little gentle
stroke too. 'It's very nice and smooth, isn't

it?' she said. 'Only don't worry about getting me one,' she added hastily. 'We've got loads of our own at home.'

'Well, Jellybean,' said Tilly's dad when Tilly got home. 'Have you found your special friend yet?'

Tilly shook her head. Her face felt stiff all over from being so polite. 'Not yet, Daddy.'

So after that, every day until school started again, Tilly's mum or dad took her to visit everyone they knew who had children the same age as Tilly.

And every time Dad asked her afterwards, 'Well, Jellybean? Have you found that friend yet?'

And Tilly would shake her head forlornly. 'Not yet, Daddy.'

The trouble was, Tilly *knew* she'd never find her special best friend this way.

But how could she tell Mum and Dad? They were only trying to help her stop being left out and lonely the best way they knew how. It wasn't *their* fault Tilly felt even lonelier and more left out than ever after every awful visit. Besides, Tilly's mum and dad were having so much fun visiting everyone. She'd never *seen* them so chatty and cheerful as they were on these outings. She didn't want to spoil things for them.

Then one day Dad took her to visit a girl called Amy. Dad was terribly cheerful again all the time they were out. Tilly kept popping hopefully downstairs to see if it was time to leave, but Dad was roaring with happy laughter, having such a good time talking to Amy's dad she thought she'd better go away again.

'So how did you like Amy?' Dad asked her as he drove her home.

'She collects cactuses,' Tilly said. She pulled a face.

'*Cacti*,' corrected dad. 'That's not so strange, is it?' he asked. 'Lots of children

collect things.
Tom collected
stamps once.'
'Amy's got
hundreds of them,'
said Tilly darkly,
'And some of
them are very
peculiar.
One's got
long hair
like a Barbie doll. Amy combs and washes it
and blows it dry with a hairdrier.
Every day.'

'That does sound strange,' Dad
admitted. Then he said sadly, 'We haven't
had much luck really, Jellybean, have we?'

'No,' agreed Tilly. 'But thank you for
trying, Daddy,' she added in a firm voice.

'Does that mean you want us to stop the
friend hunt?' asked her dad.

Tilly took a deep, brave breath. 'Yes,

please, Daddy.'

Dad sighed. 'Well, what do you know,' he murmured.

Tilly could see his face in the driving-mirror. It had a strange expression on it. A rather twitchy one. Tilly was afraid he was trying not to cry.

She patted his shoulder. 'I'm so sorry, Daddy,' she said softly. 'Are you very, very disappointed?'

Dad made a funny choking sound. To her surprise Tilly saw that he was *laughing*.

'Oh dear, Jellybean, Amy's dad is the most boring man I've met in my life,' said Dad, wiping his eyes. 'I was dying to go home all afternoon, but you kept beetling back upstairs before I could catch your eye. I thought you were having a wonderful time!'

Tilly giggled, 'Ooh, Daddy, that's because you seemed as if *you* loved it at Amy's house.'

'Never mind,' said Dad as they parked the car. 'Maybe going back to school won't be as bad as you think.'

'Yes, it will,' Tilly told him softly.

That night Sophie's friend Rose came round.

'Go away,' said Sophie, seeing Tilly hanging round the door. 'We're doing homework.'

'Boys again,' sighed Tilly.

'We've got a brilliant way to find boyfriends this term,' Rose told her. 'It's foolproof. Computer dating. It tells you all about it in my magazine.'

'What's "computer dating"?' asked Tilly.

'The computer does the difficult part,' Rose told her. 'You just feed it the information. Hobbies, favourite records, your height, the colour of your eyes and hair, and abracadabra! It finds a boyfriend that's just right for you. They have so many people to choose from, you see, that's why it works. When we get back to school, Sophie and me are trying it right away.'

Tilly's eyes grew very round and very green. She ran across the room and gave Rose a big kiss.

'Thank you, Rose,' she said gratefully. 'Thank you very *very* much.'

Then she rushed out of the room.

'What was that for?' asked Rose, surprised.

'Oh, no,' groaned Sophie, 'I know that look. Tilly's up to something.'

Next morning, Dad found Tilly in the garage, tying coloured ribbons to a rusty old mangle he'd been meaning to take to the rubbish tip. She was humming to herself.

'You look busy, Jellybean,' he said. Don't put your fingers near those big rollers, will you?'

'I'm not *silly*,' said Tilly. 'This isn't a finger-burger machine, you know.' She giggled and carried on tying ribbons

and humming.

'You seem happy today,'
said Dad. 'Have your troubles
blown away in the night?'

'Yes, they have,' said Tilly happily. 'Do
you know why, Daddy? It's because of my
special machine I invented. Look, I've made
a sign to tell about it.' She pointed.

'MATILDA BEANY'S AMAZING BEST FRIEND MACHINE,' read Dad. 'ONLY 10p – My word, Tilly. I don't think I've heard of a Best Friend Machine before.'

'I know,' said Tilly, beaming. 'That's why it says "Amazing".'

'What are all these pictures everywhere?'

'They're the Best Friends,' explained Tilly. 'I chose the friendliest ones. Do you like my one I'm getting?' She pointed at a little girl in a rainbow-patterned jumper.

'I remember buying that card for Kate years ago,' said Dad, fingering the picture of the smiling little girl. 'And that little boy is in a soap commercial, isn't he? I don't think I *quite* understand how your machine works, though, Jellybean. How are you planning to get all these perfect little children to turn up in our garage?'

'Actually, I'm in too much of a hurry to talk just at the moment, Daddy,' said Tilly swiftly. She was untangling some old branches Kate had painted silver for decorations one Christmas. 'I'm going back to school tomorrow, you see,' she explained. 'It's a good thing I thought of my invention.'

She began to fix the silver branches on top of the mangle, where they stuck out jauntily like reindeer antlers.

Tilly's dad went off to work looking thoughtful.

When Tilly didn't come back indoors at lunchtime Kate and Sophie went to see what she was up to.

They found her putting the finishing touches to her invention. Colin, the little boy from across the street, was watching. So was Colin's dog, Dimbleby.

'Go away,' said Tilly crossly to her sisters.

'I haven't got time to talk. Colin's going to try my machine, aren't you?' She beamed at him.

Colin mumbled something. Colin never got excited about anything except food. Nor did Dimbleby.

'I like the moons and stars you've stuck everywhere,' said Kate.

'They're so the children know this machine is specially important,' said Tilly.

'What about the mop and the umbrella and that wiggly bit of hose?' asked Sophie.

Tilly sighed. 'Don't you understand about machines, Sophie?' she said impatiently. 'They need *loads* of twiddly bits. They won't work without them.'

'But what do the antlers do?'

'Go away, Sophie,' snapped Tilly. 'I haven't got time to answer silly questions. I've got all the names to write out and the children's hobbies and everything.'

'The names of the friends,' explained

Colin unexpectedly. 'You have to pay ten pence, then you get a special friend of your own.'

'I saw,' said Sophie. 'That's very cheap.'

Tilly ignored her. 'Tell me your favourite hobby, Colin,' she said, beaming encouragingly. 'And I'll write it on this special paper.'

Colin looked glumly at Dimbleby's lead. 'Dunno really.'

'Don't . . . know,' Tilly wrote.

'And how tall are you?' Tilly beamed warmly at Colin again, while she waited to write down his reply.

'Dunno.'

Tilly licked her pencil. 'Don't . . . know,' she muttered. 'What's your favourite record – no, what's your favourite *dinner*, Colin?' she asked cunningly.

'Liver and onions and rice pudding,' he said at once.

Tilly sighed. 'You might not get a very

exciting friend,' she warned.

'I don't care,' said Colin. 'I've got to go home for lunch anyway.'

'You'll come back though, won't you?' asked Tilly anxiously.

But Colin was sniffing the air like a child in a gravy commercial. So was Dimbleby.

'Sausages,' said Colin, closing his eyes with pleasure. 'My mum makes bread sauce with sausages.'

And Colin and Dimbleby trotted hungrily back across the street.

'There's no one left to try my invention now.' Tilly's voice was very small. She bit her lip and twiddled her hair unhappily round her finger.

'Never mind,' Kate comforted. 'Come and have your lunch, Tilly.'

'I *do* mind. This type of machine needs loads of people, or it won't work.'

Tilly's chin wobbled violently. She scrubbed fiercely at her eyes.

'Tilly,' said Sophie, suddenly understanding, 'is your machine a kind of computer?'

'Yes,' said Tilly, suddenly sniffing hard. 'It's a very good one, actually. But the problem is there's only me and Colin to tell it stuff, and now Colin's gone home, there's only me. Well, *that's* not enough for Best Friend Machine, is it?' Her voice ended in a wail. A tear splashed on her shoe, followed by another.

Kate and Sophie looked at each other helplessly.

'That's not *quite* the only problem, Tilly,' explained Kate gently. 'You see, you can't *really* make a computer out of an old mangle. Computers are very complicated –' She stopped. Tilly's face was white and her bottom lip was trembling dangerously.

'But they're also terribly boring,' Kate added quickly. 'And they don't know the first thing about friends or magic. What you've invented, Tilly, isn't actually a boring old *computer* at all. You've made something much much more exciting.'

Left-over tears kept trickling down Tilly's face but Kate could tell she was listening.

'You've made a *MAGIC* machine,' Kate went on. 'Look,' she said, tenderly touching a dangling moon. 'It's beautiful, Tilly. Computers might be clever and complicated, but they're never ever beautiful. Your machine is full of magic hopes and wishes. Computers never have even the tiniest sprinkle of magic in them.'

'But I don't know how to make the magic work properly,' wept Tilly. 'That's the problem. I've hoped and wished for ages and ages, Kate, but nothing happens. *Nobody* wants me to be their special friend and I'm going to be left out and lonely for ever and ever.'

'Tilly,' said Sophie sternly. 'Don't you know *anything* about magic?'

Tilly glared through her tears. 'What did you say?' she demanded, in a voice that was scratchy with crossness and wobbly with misery at the same time.

'Magic doesn't always work right away,' Kate explained. 'That's what Sophie means. Remember when we helped Jess make bread? To start with it was just flour and water and crumbly old yeast.'

Tilly felt hungry remembering the smell of Jess's bread baking in the oven but she still couldn't understand what making bread had to do with magic. 'Bread isn't magic,' she objected. 'It tells you how to make it in a bread book. But I haven't got a magic book to do magic out of, you know.' And she sniffed, a long shuddery sniff that went all

114

the way down to her tummy, and more tears came leaking out.

'But magic *is* the same,' insisted Kate. 'You have to believe in it so much you *make* it come true. If you didn't believe that crumbly old yeast was going to work, you'd never even start to make bread, would you? You wouldn't go to the shop to buy the flour or wait while the bread grew and grew in its bowl by the fire.'

'Oh,' said Tilly, almost understanding now.

She felt a tiny bit hopeful suddenly. 'Is the magic I put into my machine like that yeast stuff, then?'

'Yes,' said Sophie and Kate together.

'You can't see it,' Kate added. 'But I bet you anything you like, it's already starting to work.'

Tilly looked thoughtful for a second. Then she said, 'I've been thinking. My invention isn't a Best Friend Machine any more. I've changed it. Now it's an Amazing Wishing Machine for all the Beanys.'

So after lunch Kate and Sophie helped Tilly finish her Amazing Wishing Machine.

Kate helped Tilly write down her best wishes:

A funny little kitten of her own.
A special friend to play pretending games with.
And a new house for the Beanys with apple trees to climb.

Then Sophie mangled the wishes carefully through the rollers of the Wishing Machine so Tilly wouldn't squash her fingers.

Kate and Sophie made wishes too. Tilly wasn't allowed to know what they were, so they were probably about boys. Then Colin and Dimbleby came to join in. Tilly said they could have a wish each. Colin didn't say his and Dimbleby's wishes out loud but Tilly bet *they* were about bread sauce and bones. Then Mum and Tom had a go.

'The yeasty magic is working,' said Tilly happily. 'You can't see it, but it is.' She sniffed the frosty air. 'I can smell it actually.'

'What are you Beanys doing out here in the cold?' said Dad, surprising them. His coat was buttoned up to his chin and there didn't seem to be nearly as much room inside it as usual.

'Hurray, you're early,' said Tilly. 'You can do a wish in my magic machine, Daddy.'

'Dad, what's wriggling inside your coat?' asked Tom suddenly.

Dad laughed, unfastening his top button. A pair of furry ears shot out of his collar, followed by a skinny black hooky paw. Then a cross little face with round yellow eyes and long shining whiskers, popped up under Dad's chin, squeaking loudly.

'A kitten,' shouted Kate and Sophie.

'And they aren't very easy to find this

time of year, believe me,' said Dad, unhooking the kitten's claws from his shoulder.

'Those eyes,' said Mum, stroking the kitten's tiny black head. 'They're like headlamps!'

'Do you think this little creature could be your friend while you're waiting for that really special one, Tilly?' Dad asked anxiously. 'Ow – let's call him Spike. His claws are like needles!'

But Tilly still couldn't say a word.

Her Wishing Machine was really magic!

And now, like the crumbly yeast, the magic had started to work.

Tilly Vanilla and the House Cooling

But having a kitten in the family wasn't a bit how Tilly thought it would be.

'You did wish for a funny kitten,' said Kate when Tilly showed her the angry scratches on her hand next day. 'And he *is* funny!'

'I meant funny-nice,' said Tilly, sucking her hand. 'Not funny-fierce or funny-peculiar.'

Spike went racing up the living-room curtains, couldn't get down again and hung upside down like a bat, noisily demanding to be rescued.

'Serves you right,' said Tilly. 'So ha-ha to you. Stay there until you

119

say sorry.'

But Spike didn't know how to be sorry. And he didn't know how to be fluffy, cosy and sweet like the kitten Mum had had when she was little. The Beanys' kitten was wriggly, glossy, skinny and *very* small; except his ears, which were huge, like furry satellite dishes. With his yellow headlamp-eyes he looked more like a space creature than a baby animal.

Spike didn't behave even a little bit the way kittens were meant to behave. He was too wriggly and bitey to sit on Tilly's knee and purr while she stroked and sang songs to him. And he was far too wriggly to ride peacefully in the doll's pram like the cat Tilly's mum had had.

Spike preferred rough, tough, bouncy games. He liked galloping sideways at Tilly like a tiny circus pony. And he liked playing gangsters, lying in wait until Tilly went upstairs, then grabbing at her ankles with his spiky paws like a prickly handcuff.

Spike didn't even know how to make proper kitten noises. When he was cross, Spike humped his back and spat like the steam iron and did tiny growly noises in his throat. He didn't mew, he squeaked like a rusty hinge in the wind, and when he purred (which he did when the Beanys had chicken or tuna for supper) he sounded like the telephone dialling tone.

Spike didn't understand that his basket was meant for sleeping in either. He thought it was for playing 'Capture the Castle'. When he felt tired he crept into the smelly old cupboard under the sink with the bucket and scrubbing brush, or climbed into the ironing basket and slept there instead.

Once Spike actually had his forty

winks in the dressing-up box! Tilly thought he was a furry hat until he opened one cross yellow eye and squeaked his rusty squeak at her.

'You're a bit mixed up, *I* think,' Tilly told him, when she'd got over her fright.

There was something else the Beanys' kitten was mixed up about.

Spike didn't know he was meant to be Tilly's special friend. The new kitten liked Tom best. It just wasn't fair.

Until Tilly's brother came home from school, Spike played his gangster games quite happily with Tilly; chasing traily bits of wool, and scrumpled sweet papers. But the moment Tom walked through the door, the kitten rushed round after *him*, just as if Tilly wasn't there.

Spike liked to ride around on Tom's

shoulder like a parrot. (When Tilly tried, her shoulders were too small. Spike dug his claws in wildly, trying not to fall off, and it was very horrible for both of them.)

At bedtime, when Mum wasn't looking, Spike sneaked into Tom and Tilly's room and curled up in Tom's bed. Tilly knew because she woke in the night and heard the happy telephone noises on the other side of the room.

How did Spike bear the sock smell?

Tom didn't even *need* a special friend. He already had weird Merv. Tilly was the left-out, lonely one.

But Tilly still tried to go on believing that her Wishing Machine was secretly working its magic, the way Kate said. Probably it was easier for it to make the littler things like kittens come true first, she told herself bravely.

Tilly tried to be brave about school too. At least this term they were doing volcanoes instead of best friends. Miss Hinchin stuck volcano pictures round the classroom. The children made their own volcanoes out of *papier-mâché*. They wrote a poem together with words like 'erupt' and 'lava' in it and acted it out in assembly for the whole school.

At playtime Bernice and Stephanie played together now. They didn't play pretending games, they had crazes. The first craze was for tying floppy bits of elastic round their ankles and doing a specially complicated kind of jumping.

But by the time Tilly's mum remembered to buy Tilly some elastic, Bernice and Stephanie were doing Knitting Nancies instead and everyone at school had joined the knitting craze.

Some people's Knitting Nancies were smart ones from the toy shop. Other people made them out of old cotton spools. Sophie gave Tilly her old one. You had to slip loops

of coloured wool over the nails.
A snake of knitted wool was
meant to grow down inside
your cotton reel and come out
the other end. Tilly couldn't do
it for toffee. She ended up with
a messy tangle every time.

Bernice and Stephanie always went
off their crazes as soon as the other
children copied them and once Bernice
and Stephanie were bored with a
craze, the fun somehow went out of
it. It was only what *they* were doing
that seemed exciting to everyone.

One week everybody was mad
about making pompoms for babies.
Then it was skipping.
Then, just before the
Easter holidays, it
was Lucky Bags.

LUCKY
BAG

'But I always get the *unlucky* bags, that's the trouble,' sighed Tilly, walking to school with Kate and Ollie one day. She was nearly used to Ollie Pyke now, though on Tuesdays and Thursdays she had to be careful which side of him she walked, because of being banged in the leg by his art folder. Ollie had art on those days. He planned to be an artist when he left school.

'Stephanie and Bernice get lovely things. I only get yucky sweets like painted Rice Krispies and muddly plastic figures that you can't see what they're meant to be.'

'I remember those bags. They look so exciting on the outside,' sympathised Kate. 'I never got anything nice in them either.'

'They cost *loads* of money,' said Tilly sadly.

'Don't buy them then,' said sensible Ollie.

Tilly knew he was right, but she couldn't stop hoping that one day she'd buy a *really* lucky Lucky Bag. Tilly wasn't asking much, was she? Just a real Lucky Bag and a real friend to play real games with, instead of silly crazes that made her feel left out when she didn't join in, and bored or stupid when she did.

But that evening something so amazing happened that friends and Lucky Bags flew right out of Tilly's mind.

'We're going to look at a house,' Dad told them at supper. 'We've found one we can afford at last.'

Tilly was so shocked she breathed her mashed potato in, instead of swallowing it. 'You mean, we're leaving our own little house?' she said as soon as she could talk again.

'But I love this house so much,' wailed Kate.

Mum laughed. 'You always said you hated it!'

'We're used to it,' declared Sophie. 'It fits

us Beanys snugly like a grungy old sock.'

'Not one of Tom's though,' shuddered Tilly.

Dad picked up Tilly's foot in its spotty, shrunken sock and wiggled it on his knee. One of her toes peeped out the end. Dad drew a little Tilly face on it with a biro while Tilly giggled.

'This house fits the Beanys a bit *too* snuggly,' he said, when he'd finished his drawing. 'We're bursting out, like Tilly's toes. Anyway, come and see what we've found. It isn't grand and it needs lots of work doing to it, but it's quite special.'

'It isn't in the country, is it?' asked Sophie suspiciously.

'It's bang in the middle of town,' said Mum. 'Much nearer the shops.'

'And everyone can have their own room,' said Dad. 'There's even a spare one for you, Spike!'

Spike sleepily opened one yellow headlamp a tiny crack.

'Daddy's just joking, Spike,' Tilly explained.

The Beanys piled into the car without even doing the washing-up and drove into the very middle of town. Tilly felt a bit sick. In her excitement she'd gobbled her tea and it felt too near the top for safety.

'This is it,' said Mum, parking the car. 'And nobody's to say a word until you've seen the garden.'

No one did, but Tilly knew what everyone was thinking. This house was a *dump*.

It was thin and gloomy like a dark skinny finger, with a sticky-out window in the roof. The paint was peeling. The gate was hanging off. Sweet papers had blown into the front garden and forgotten to blow out again.

Tilly opened her mouth in horror.

'Not a word,' said Mum firmly. 'Not a *word*.'

She unfastened a shabby gate.

'Won't the people mind?' asked Kate nervously.

'It's empty,' said Mum. 'We've got the key.'

Everyone trailed silently after her up the alley. It was like being in a dark, spooky tunnel.

'But I don't –' Tilly began. Only she never finished what she was going to say because all at once the tunnel ended. She was in a twilit garden under a lilac tree and birds were singing all around her.

'Oh, it's amazing,' whispered Kate.

'It's just like the country,' said Tom.

'Hey, this is cool,' said Sophie.

There was still enough light to see by. The evening was full of the scent of lilacs. A blackbird sang from the washing post. Another blackbird answered over and over from a tree two doors down. Old-fashioned chimneys stood out sharply against the pink and gold sky like the crowns of kings and queens.

At the bottom of the overgrown garden a cat made its way along the high wall. It jumped over the broken place in the bricks where next door's rose bush was creeping in.

'It's a bit of a mess . . .' began Dad

apologetically.

But Tilly had suddenly seen the apple trees. 'Oh, I don't believe it,' she shouted. 'Just like a little magic wood!'

And she ran through the long wet grass until she was standing right under the trees. They leaned over her like a green tent. If she stood on tiptoe she could just touch the freckly blossom. All at once she heard a soft whispering sound and looked round sharply to see who was talking.

Tilly's neck prickled, as if someone nearby was watching the Beanys explore the overgrown garden. But she couldn't see anyone. It must just be the trees whispering. Tilly couldn't catch what they were saying but for some reason she didn't feel nearly so lonely.

'You're there, aren't you?' Tilly said softly. 'You're somewhere very, very near.'

Suddenly she saw something in the grass. A pair of plastic sunglasses. Tilly tried

them on and they fitted as if they'd been
made for her. They made everything
look pink.

Tilly peered around the pink dusky
garden beaming to herself. She knew she
was going to meet the owner of the
sunglasses very soon.

'We're going to poke about inside while
we can still see,' called Mum.

But Tilly wanted to stay in the pink

garden for a while.

Then, before she followed the others indoors, she put the glasses back carefully where she'd found them, in case their owner needed them in a hurry.

The house was bare and empty inside, not crowded and homey like their own house. The walls were covered in dark ugly paper and the kitchen smelled of old tea leaves and school cabbage. But Mum promised they'd make it beautiful in time and because of the whispering apple trees, Tilly believed her.

'So do we agree?' asked Tilly's dad.

And they did. The Beanys were moving house at last!

Next day, Tilly told Miss Hinchin.

Miss Hinchin said, 'You'll have to have a housewarming, Tilly.'

'Oh, it's not cold,' said Tilly quickly. 'It's got huge radiators and everything.'

Miss Hinchin explained that a

134

housewarming was a special party to celebrate moving into a new house.

When she got home Tilly told her mum that the Beanys had to have a housewarming if they were going to do the moving properly.

But Mum was frazzled with lists and telephone calls. 'By the time we get things organised it'll be summer,' she told Tilly in despair.

'That's all right,' said Tilly brightly. 'We'll have a house *cooling* instead.'

Her mum laughed. 'You see everything through rose-coloured glasses, Tilly,' she said, hugging her.

Tilly was surprised Mum knew about the glasses. But remembering the friendly feeling in the garden, she suddenly hugged herself hard.

'Penny for your thoughts,' said Kate.

Tilly's thoughts were too complicated to put into words so she stroked Spike instead. He rolled on to his back, all four skinny black paws in the air like a spider, and chewed her wrist.

'There's other cats to play gangsters with at the new house,' Tilly told him. 'And trees to climb instead of our curtains.'

Before the new people moved in, the Beanys had to take all their old rubbish to the dump. Dad said Tilly's invention really had to go, and there was to be No Fuss, so sadly she went to say goodbye one last time.

But she saw at once that all the invention's magic had been used right up. Tilly's Amazing Wishing Machine was only a rusty old mangle again. Tilly lovingly unfastened the moons and stars and peeled off the pictures of the smiling, perfect, special best friends.

Then she untied the ribbons and lifted down the silver-painted antlers.

'Clever old you,' she whispered. 'You magicked the kitten and you magicked the Beanys a whole new house.'

Probably the machine had used all the magic up before it got to the best friend part, she thought sadly. Magicking a kitten mightn't use a lot, but a house was bound to use loads. And Tilly didn't want to be greedy, like *The Old Woman Who Lived in the Vinegar Bottle*.

So she patted the rusty mangle and left without saying a word about her other wishes.

When the removal men arrived, Tilly and Spike hid on the stairs, then they hid under the table until it was time for the

table to be carried out to the
van with the rest
of the furniture.

Spike had to
go in his special
basket. His
yellow eyes
were so big
with fright
he looked
more like a
space creature than ever.

'Don't worry,' Tilly comforted him as
the men tramped to and fro. 'I'll look after
you.'

Suddenly the Beanys' little house was
empty. It was time to go.

'Hey,' said Tom. 'Guess what – I've
found my penknife I lost ages ago.'

'Goodbye, house,' said Sophie tearfully.
'Don't forget us.'

'It's a new beginning,' said Dad.

'A brand-new beginning for the Beanys.'

Tilly slipped her hand in his. She liked it when Dad said that. It made her feel as if she was living in a story that just had to come right in the end.

Colin and Dimbleby came out of their house to wave goodbye.

'Did my machine magic *your* wish, Colin?' Tilly called as they drove away. Dimbleby grinned and wagged his tail at her but Colin was chewing a lump of fruit cake and didn't hear.

When the Beanys arrived at the new house, Tilly ran into the garden right away. She wanted to stay outdoors until the rooms stopped looking so strange and messy.

She pottered down through the overgrown grass in the sunshine. A fat bee buzzed past her ear. It was so hot the daisies had opened their petals out flat like tiny plates. Tilly picked one of the flowers, jabbing her nail into its juicy stalk. She

could make a daisy chain
MILES long if she wanted. There
were millions.

Then she heard a voice murmuring
on the other side of the wall, slightly
muffled, as if someone was talking into
their hand.

Tilly began to run, because she
couldn't wait any longer. She really
couldn't wait to meet the friend she'd
been wishing and hoping for for so
long. It was truly amazing of the
Wishing Machine, she thought, to
magic a house *and* a special friend so
cleverly in one go. Tilly could never
have thought of it in a thousand years!

She hunted around in the grass. Yes!
The pink sunglasses were still there. She
picked them up and tiptoed over to the
broken part of the garden wall.

The murmuring was louder now but
still strangely muffled.

Tilly peered into next door's garden, her heart thudding.

Someone had made a tent out of a blanket draped across a wooden clothes airer. The blanket wiggled about wildly as if there wasn't quite enough room inside. Once a bare foot shot underneath it, and quickly shot back again.

The foot was exactly the same size as Tilly's own, only browner.

Tilly shivered and hugged herself for luck. She took a big breath. 'Hallo,' she called. 'I'm Tilly Beany. And I've found your glasses in the grass. I expect you want them back, don't you?'

The murmuring stopped abruptly. The blanket tent heaved with surprise. The airer fell over with a thud.

'Ow,' complained an invisible someone. 'That hurt.'

'It wasn't my fault,' yelled someone else.

The blanket heaved again. Tilly swallowed.

141

She'd been wrong again. There wasn't just ONE someone under there, a lonely left-out little girl like Tilly. There were TWO girls, playing happily together, like Bernice and Stephanie.

Tilly's eyes prickled. She began to walk slowly back towards the house. 'One is one and all alone and ever more shall be so,' she whispered to herself.

'Hey!' yelled someone. 'Hey, Tilly thingy. Don't go.'

Tilly sighed. 'Sorry,' she was going to say. 'I didn't mean to spoil your game.'

But when she turned round she got a shock. No wonder there wasn't much room in the tent. There were *three* girls staring back at her! They looked hot from being under the blanket, and rather surprised from having the airer fall over. There was a freckly girl with short brown hair, and a bright rainbow T-shirt. There was a long, leggedy girl wearing a dressing-up hat with a huge rose on it. She was the person whose foot Tilly had seen first. The third girl had silky-soft fair hair flopping unevenly all over her face and she wore a big, baggy denim dress that nearly reached her ankles.

All three girls were as different from each other as it was possible for people to be.

And all three girls were smiling back at Tilly.

'I found some sunglasses,' said Tilly shyly.

'Oh, they're mine,' said the girl with the hat. 'I used to play in your garden when no one lived there. I couldn't remember where I left them so Mum bought some new ones.

Keep those if you like.'

'Oh,' said Tilly surprised. 'Thank you.'
She put them on. Everyone giggled. Then
she took them off again.

'Well – bye,' she said awkwardly. 'We're
just moving in so it's a bit busy you see.'

'Oh come on, stay and play,' said the
freckly one. 'I'm Nessa.'

'And I'm Emily,' said the one in the hat.
'I'm the one who lives here. These two live
down the street.'

'I'm Beth,' said the third. Beth shook her
raggedy silk hair out of her eyes and Tilly
saw to her amazement that they were as
blue as cornflowers.

'We've got a club,' said Beth. 'It would
be miles better with four. Do you want to be
in it too, Tilly?'

Tilly had never dreamed she'd be asked
to join a club in a million years!

'Is it a secret one?' she asked at once.
'Do I have to swear not to tell anyone and

have you got a code no one else can understand? And a hollow tree to keep the rules in?'

Emily giggled. 'I told you she looked fun,' she said to the others. 'We saw you ages ago,' she explained. 'When you came to look round. But we hid until we knew what you were like.'

'I know,' said Tilly remembering. 'But I thought there was only one of you.'

It was amazing. She'd asked the Wishing Machine for one friend, because of the Best Friend Project and not being in a two like Noah's Ark, and here were *three*! One wearing rainbow colours, one in a dressing-up hat, and one with eyes of cornflower blue, so there was no doubt these girls were Tilly's special friends that she'd been longing for all this time.

Now she'd met them Tilly wondered how she could ever have thought just one friend would be enough. Having three was going to be three times as much fun!

'Climb over the wall,' said Emily. 'My mum's defrosting the freezer and she says we can finish up all the ice cream. Let's have an ice cream party.'

'No,' said Tilly excitedly. 'Bring it over here instead. I'll tell you why, Emily, so it can be a proper HOUSE COOLING party.'

There was an enormous amount of ice cream. Emily's mum brought it out in a huge bowl with all the different kinds muddled together and there was a spoon for everyone.

'I like the pink sort best,' said Emily, from under her big hat.

'I like the toffee one,' said Beth, blowing her raggedy hair out of her eyes. Beth had an ice cream moustache now.

'Vanilla's my best,' said Tilly slurping happily. 'Do you know why?'

'Why?' the others asked, puzzled.

But Tilly didn't get the chance to explain because someone came wheeling his squeaky, creaky old bike down the alley and a voice called, 'Anyone at home?'

'It's Ollie!' shouted Tilly.

'I've come to lend the Beanys a hand,' Ollie explained. 'And I've got something for you, Tilly. I made you a little housewarming present.'

'House *cooling* you mean,' Tilly corrected, giggling. Then she looked in astonishment at what Ollie had given her. 'Oh, *Ollie*,' she whispered.

It was much bigger than the Lucky Bags in the sweet shop. Ollie had painted it the inky blue colour of the sky and decorated the bag all over with suns, moons and stars. All around it was silvery magic-looking writing.

TILLY BEANY'S TRULY AMAZING AND FANTASTIC LUCKY BAG, said the silver writing on the inky cloth.

Tilly nearly forgot to breathe.

'Go on, open it,' said Ollie. 'There isn't one single painted Rice Krispy in it, honest.'

The bag fastened with a beautiful rainbow-coloured ribbon.

'My fingers are

too excited,' said Tilly shakily. Somehow she got the bag undone.

Everyone watched as she reached into the bag and pulled out the first surprise.

A fat silver felt-tip pen for doing wizard's writing!

'That's for the secret code,' she told the others.

Next came a little notebook with ripply coloured patterns on it, the kind petrol makes in a rain puddle. 'That's for putting our rules in,' said Tilly.

Third came a magnifying glass.

'That's for spying with, isn't it?' said Nessa.

There were sweets, too. Four fat toffees in shiny coloured paper.

'How did you know, Ollie?' asked Tilly, astonished. She shared the sweets out right away, one each for everyone.

Next came a funny badge with a grinning kitten on it, a pearly shell, and last of all a ring with a stone that changed colour mysteriously when Tilly put it on.

'Pretend that's our treasure,' said Tilly at once. 'And we have to keep it safe.'

She shook the bag hopefully but it was quite empty now so she jumped up and gave Ollie a big hug. Ollie Pyke didn't look even a *little* bit like a stick insect, now she'd got to know him properly.

'Better eat your ice cream before it melts,' said Ollie. 'I didn't mean to interrupt your party.'

'Oh, yes, I was telling them why vanilla's my best ice cream,' Tilly remembered, giggling.

'And why is it?' asked Ollie. He was laughing too, even though he didn't know what the joke was yet.

'You've got to guess!' said Tilly. She

beamed around at them.

'I think *I* know,' said Beth slowly.

'So do I,' said Nessa giggling.

'And I do,' said Emily, fanning herself with her hat.

'Well, I wish someone would tell ME,' said Ollie, pretending to be hurt.

'It's easy,' said Nessa. 'It's because – *vanilla* –' she dropped her voice to a whisper as if she was going to tell a big secret. Then she stopped instead and pointed to Emily.

'– rhymes with –' Emily continued, giggling and then *she* pointed to Beth.

'*Her*!' Beth finished. And *they* all pointed at Tilly.

'Tilly Vanilla!' shouted Tilly. 'Do you get it, Ollie? And these are my three special best friends anyway and this is the best house cooling party ever. And this is the best day in my life. So there!'

And it was.

Other titles starring Tilly Beany

The Real Tilly Beany
Annie Dalton
Illustrated by Kate Sheppard

Tilly Beany Saves the World
Annie Dalton
Illustrated by Kate Sheppard

EGMONT
We bring stories to life